W9-BXE-806

DRAGONBLOOD

EYE OF THE MONSTER

BY MICHAEL DAHL

ILLUSTRATED BY
FEDERICO PIATTI

STONE ARCH BOOKS
a capstone imprint

Zone Books are published by
Stone Arch Books
A Capstone Imprint
151 Good Counsel Drive, P.O. Box 669
Mankato, Minnesota 56002
www.capstonepub.com

Printed in the United States of America in North Mankato, Minnesota.
092009
005618CGS10

Library of Congress Cataloging-in-Publication Data is available on the Library of Congress website.

Library binding: 978-1-4342-1928-2

Art Director: Kay Fraser
Graphic Designer: Hilary Wacholz
Production Specialist: Michelle Biedscheid

6/10

TABLE OF CONTENTS

Introduction

A new Age of Dragons is about to begin. The powerful creatures will return to rule the world once more, but this time will be different. This time, they will have allies. Who will help them? Around the world, some young humans are making a strange discovery. They are learning that they were born with dragon blood – blood that gives them amazing powers.

CHAPTER 1
BLOODY

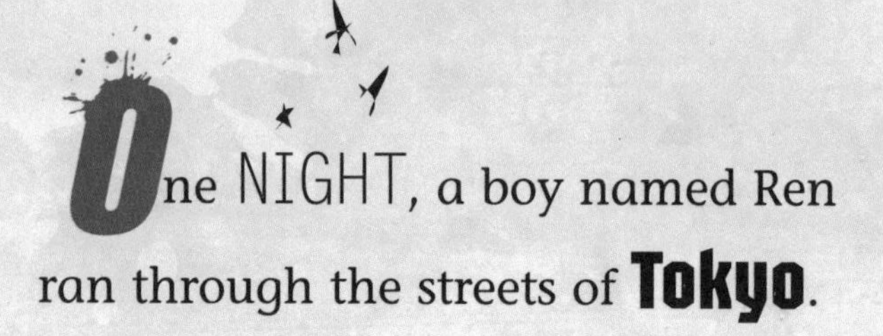

One NIGHT, a boy named Ren ran through the streets of Tokyo.

His nose was Bloody.

His clothes were torn.

A bruise darkened his cheek.

Earlier, Ren had walked out of a movie theater. He saw some other boys from his school.

The other boys were OLDER and **stronger**. They had hard muscles and cruel smiles.

They laughed because Ren was small and weak.

They knocked him around. They ripped his school uniform.

A fist flew into Ren's face and crunched his nose.

Blood spattered onto his shirt.

Harsh laughter echoed in the street as Ren ran for safety.

CHAPTER 2
THE REFLECTION

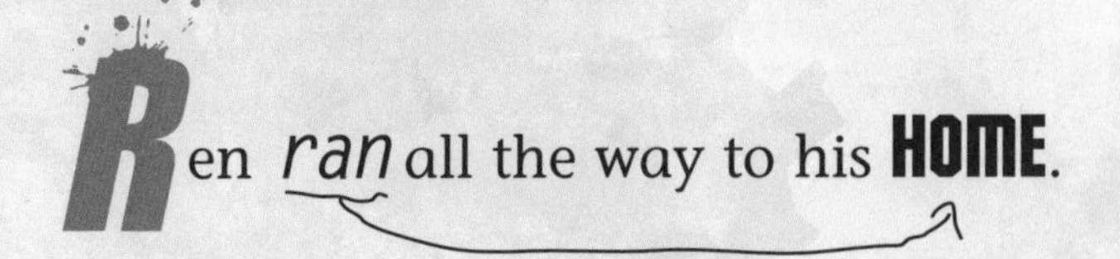

Ren ran all the way to his HOME.

He stopped OUTSIDE in the garden to catch his breath.

He kneeled down by a small pool.

His hands scooped up cold water to clean his face.

His hands trembled with anger.

The cold water could not keep his face from feeling hot.

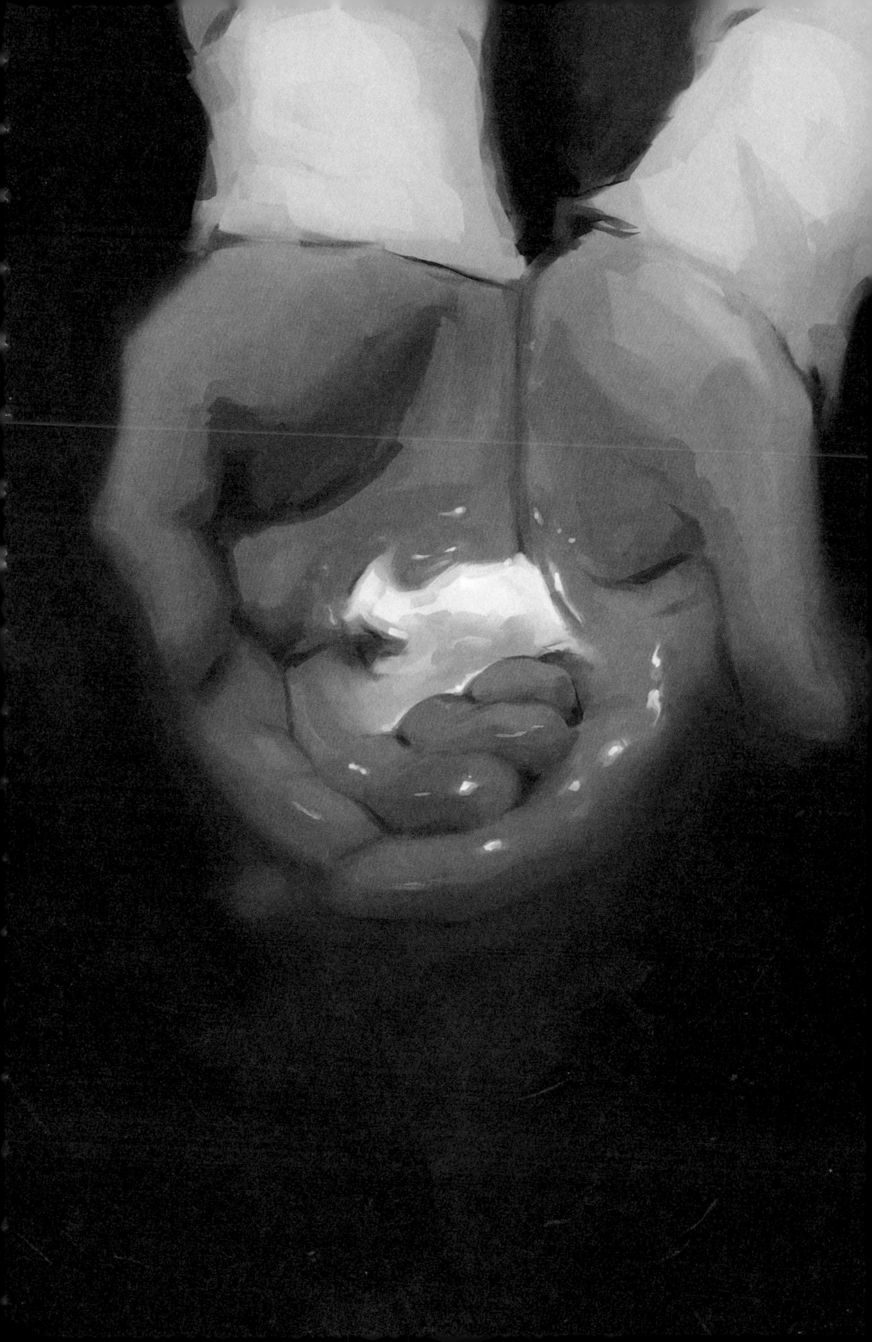

Ren leaned over and looked at himself in the pool. Light from a window lit his face.

They're right, he thought.

I am ***small*** and weak.

Why couldn't I be taller?

Why don't I have muscles like theirs?

His nose was swollen. His eyes looked red and full of FEAR.

CHAPTER 3
THE NIGHTMARE

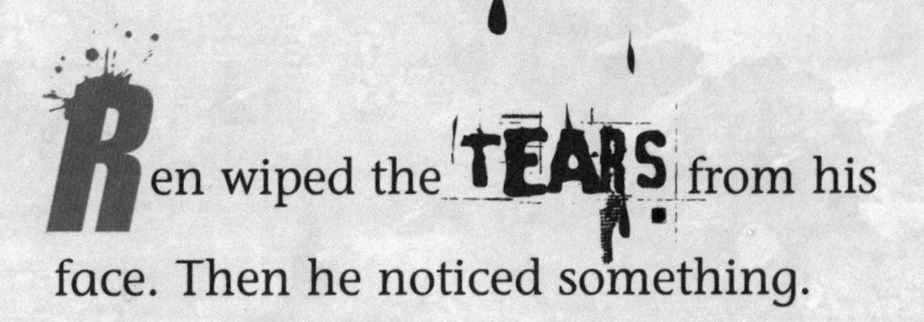

Ren wiped the TEARS from his face. Then he noticed something.

His eyes had changed color.

They were no longer brown.

Instead, they looked HUGE and golden.

The eyes reminded him of a nightmare he'd had many times.

In the dream, he turned into a giant black dragon. The nightmare dragon had burning yellow eyes.

"That was only a dream," the boy said to himself.

Then he felt a sharp pain in his back.

He stared down into the pool.

Two huge black WINGS were sprouting from his shoulders.

His eyes *gleamed* yellow.

His face turned into the face of a MONSTER. It was fierce and powerful looking. He was terrifying and strong.

"Yes!" shouted the boy.

But the word sounded like a roar coming from his new and massive throat.

Two dark wings flapped in the garden. The boy's feet, now armed with sharp talons, lifted from the grass.

The shadowy **CREATURE** turned and soared above the house.

CHAPTER 4
THE PREDATOR

A dragon flew above the bright streets of Tokyo.

The creature sniffed the air. Its yellow eyes scanned the ground, searching for prey.

Four boys laughed and joked as they walked down an alley.

A HUGE shadow dropped in front of them. The boys stopped and stared.

The powerful creature reached out a huge claw. It gripped two of the boys within its talons. The boys SCREAMED.

Then the dragon leaped into the air. The boys hung below the MONSTER, trapped in its grip.

They yelled for HELP.

"Now you'll know how it feels," screamed the dragon. His voice only sounded like a fierce ROAR.

The dragon flew higher into the evening sky.

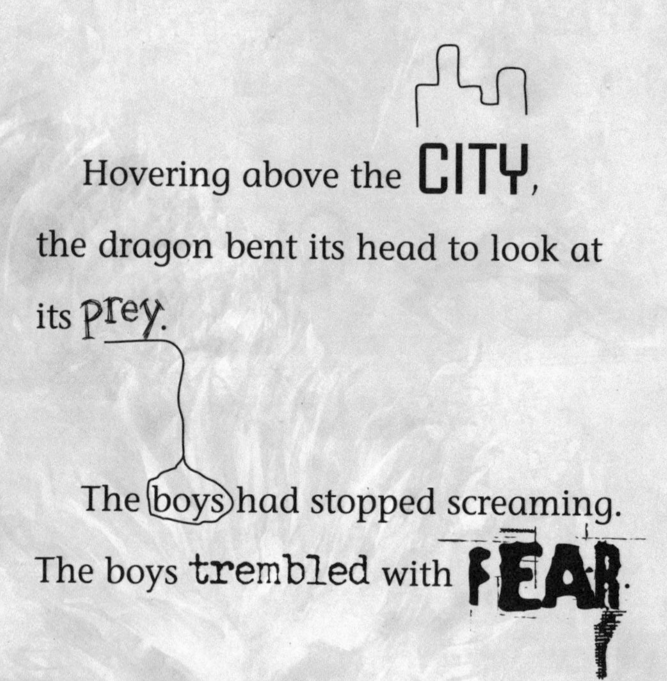

Hovering above the CITY,

the dragon bent its head to look at

its prey.

The boys had stopped screaming.

The boys trembled with FEAR.

The dragon stared into their

faces. It recognized the look in their

eyes. It was a look that the dragon

had seen in its own eyes only

minutes ago.

Swiftly, the creature flew back to the alley. It gently placed the boys on the ground. Then it soared away.

The dragon flew to a quiet garden in a DARK part of the city. It landed near a small pool. Softly, it folded its huge WINGS.

The dragon was a fierce creature, but Ren did NOT want to be a monster.

In the eye of the beholder

In 1793, a girl with one eye in the middle of her forehead was born in France. She lived to be 15.

Eye color comes from a pigment called **melanin**. Eyes that don't have any melanin are blue. Brown eyes have lots of melanin. In between blue and brown come green, hazel, gold, and sometimes violet eyes.

Most babies are born with blue eyes, but eye color continues to change and develop for a few more years. A person's eye color is usually final by three years of age. However, eye color can change due to age or disease as well.

Some people have eyes that are two different colors. This is called **heterochromia**. Demi Moore, Kiefer Sutherland, and Kate Bosworth are just a few known people with this condition.

Italian women used to put drops of juice from the poisonous belladonna plant in their eyes to enlarge their pupils. They believed this would make their eyes look brighter, enhancing their beauty.

On the inside corner of your eye is the remnant of a third eyelid. Some animals, such as reptiles, still have this protective lid after their birth.

ABOUT THE AUTHOR

Michael Dahl is the author of more than 200 books for children and young adults. He has won the AEP Distinguished Achievement Award three times for his nonfiction. His Finnegan Zwake mystery series was shortlisted twice by the Anthony and Agatha awards. He has also written the Library of Doom series. He is a featured speaker at conferences around the country on graphic novels and high-interest books for boys.

ABOUT THE ILLUSTRATOR

After getting a graphic design degree and working as a designer for a couple of years, Federico Piatti realized he was spending way too much time drawing and painting, and too much money on art books and comics, so his path took a turn towards illustration. He currently works creating imagery for books and games, mostly in the fantasy and horror genres. Argentinian by birth, he now lives in Madrid, Spain, with his wife, who is also an illustrator.

GLOSSARY

bruise (BROOZ)—a dark mark you get on your skin when you fall or are hit

creature (KREE-chur)—a living being

cruel (KROO-uhl)—mean, happy to see others suffer

darkened (DAR-kuhnd)—made darker

fierce (FEERSS)—violent, dangerous, extreme

harsh (HARSH)—cruel or rough

muscles (MUHSS-uhlz)—the parts of a body that produce movement and show strength

predator (PRED-uh-tor)—an animal that lives by hunting other animals

prey (PRAY)—an animal that is hunted by other animals

recognize (REK-uhg-nize)—to see something and know what it is

sprouting (SPROU-ting)—starting to grow

DISCUSSION QUESTIONS

1. Why were the other boys picking on Ren? What could he have done to stop them?

2. Why do you think Ren's eyes changed color? What other transformations did he go through?

3. Why didn't Ren hurt the bullies? What would you have done? Explain your answer.

WRITING PROMPTS

1. Ren doesn't want to be a **bully**. Write about a time you were bullied. What happened?

2. Were you surprised by the ending? Write a paragraph describing what you thought would happen at the end.

3. Pick one of the **characters** from the story. Then write one more chapter describing what happened to him.

WAIT!
DON'T close the book!
There's MORE!
www.capstonekids.com
Still want MORE?
Find cool websites and more books like this one at www.Facthound.com.
Just type in the Book ID: 9781434219282
and you're ready to go!